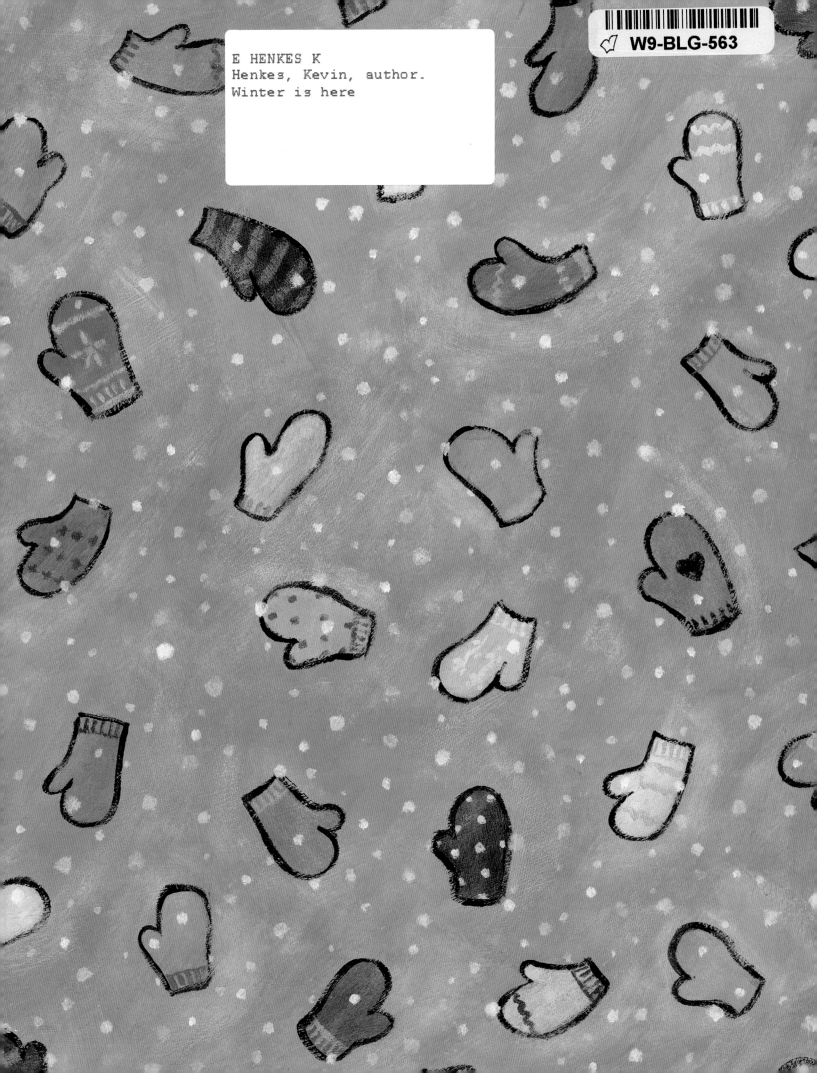

# Winter
## Is
## Here

BY Kevin Henkes

ILLUSTRATED BY Laura Dronzek

GREENWILLOW BOOKS
*An Imprint of HarperCollins Publishers*

Winter Is Here

Text copyright © 2018 by Kevin Henkes

Illustrations copyright © 2018 by Laura Dronzek

All rights reserved. Manufactured in China. For information address

HarperCollins Children's Books, a division of HarperCollins Publishers,

195 Broadway, New York, NY 10007.

www.harpercollinschildrens.com

Acrylic paints were used to prepare the full-color art.

The text type is 32-point Bernhard Gothic SG Medium.

Library of Congress Cataloging-in-Publication Data is available.

ISBN 978-0-06-274718-1 (trade ed.)—ISBN 978-0-06-274719-8 (lib. bdg.)

18 19 20 21 22 SCP 10 9 8 7 6 5 4 3 2 1

First Edition

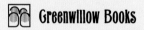

Greenwillow Books

For Will and Clara

**W**inter is here.
It's everywhere.

It's falling from the sky

and sitting on the houses

and dripping from the roofs

and sticking to the trees in clumps and curls.

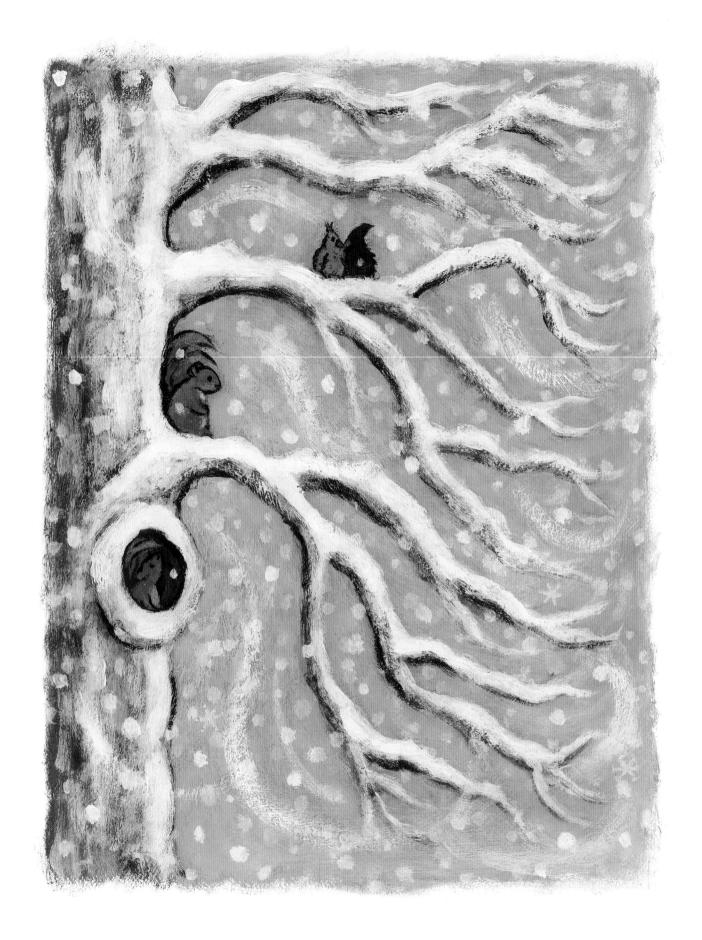

Winter is reaching through the branches

and crouching in doorways

and settling here and there
softly, so softly.

But Winter can be hard, too.
Ice covers the pond.
The leaves underneath are like stars in glass.

It can take a long time
to get ready
for Winter.

Boots and zippers

and vests and zippers

and jackets and zippers

and hats

and snaps

and scarves and mittens.

Winter is outside, of course,
but it's inside, too,

feathering the window
and dusting the dog
and sitting on the table.

Winter comes without a sound . . .

and it comes with many.

The wind howls in every language

and the windows rattle.

Winter is white and gray.

But with the dark of night,
Winter is blue.
Blue, blue, deep blue.
And even colder.

Winter comes

and then it stays

and stays

and stays,

and when it's time to leave,
Winter shrinks away bit by bit.

It slows down
getting smaller
drying up

slipping down the street
around the corner

peeking back
then moving on

out into the world
into the air, into . . .

Spring.